To my sister, Deona, who had the audacity
to be extremely adorable when she was little
—A. Z.

STERLING CHILDREN'S BOOKS
New York

An Imprint of Sterling Publishing Co., Inc.
1166 Avenue of the Americas
New York, NY 10036

ISBN 978-1-4549-2293-3

Distributed in Canada by Sterling Publishing Co., Inc.
c/o Canadian Manda Group, 664 Annette Street
Toronto, Ontario, Canada M6S 2C8
Distributed in the United Kingdom by GMC Distribution Services
Castle Place, 166 High Street, Lewes, East Sussex, BN7 1XU England
Distributed in Australia by NewSouth Books
45 Beach Street, Coogee, NSW 2034, Australia

For information about custom editions, special sales, and premium and corporate
purchases, please contact Sterling Special Sales at 800-805-5489
or specialsales@sterlingpublishing.com.

Manufactured in China

Lot #:
2 4 6 8 10 9 7 5 3 1
11/17

sterlingpublishing.com

Design by Irene Vandervoort

Marigold & Daisy

Words and Pictures by
ANDREA ZUILL

STERLING CHILDREN'S BOOKS
New York

My life was good.

Then my little sister, Daisy, was born. I immediately sensed something was wrong.

Fascination with Daisy grew as she got older.
There was something about her that seemed to
mesmerize everyone.

The situation had really gotten out of control.

I tried talking to Dad about Daisy, but it was clear he didn't understand.

I had to figure out why Daisy had such an effect on everyone. What was her plan? Then it finally dawned on me:

DAISY WAS AN EVIL GENIUS SET OUT TO CONQUER THE WORLD WITH HER POWER OF BEING EXTREMELY ADORABLE!

That had to be it. Nothing else made sense.

She must have sensed I was on to her, because all of a sudden her attention was entirely focused on me.

She invaded my personal space.

And found new ways to be annoying.

Be-bop-a-Shoobie-Doobie

Then she went too far.

I couldn't believe what Daisy had done. Mom was
no help at all.

I'd had enough!

Stop that!
How dare you talk to my sister like that! She's the bestest and greatest person ever! You need to be nice and learn some manners and...and...I know where you live!

Well, she may be an evil genius, but at least she's my evil genius.

ONE YEAR LATER . . .